To all the little Annes out there
(spelled with an *e* or not!) —K.G.

Text copyright © 2018 by Kallie George

Illustrations copyright © 2018 by Geneviève Godbout

Tundra Books, an imprint of Penguin Random House Canada Young Readers, a Penguin Random House Company

Library and Archives Canada Cataloguing in Publication

George, K. (Kallie), 1983-, author
    Goodnight, Anne / Kallie George ; Geneviève Godbout, illustrator.

Issued in print and electronic formats.
ISBN 978-1-77049-926-3 (hardcover).—ISBN 978-1-77049-927-0 (EPUB)

        I. Godbout, Geneviève, 1985-, illustrator II. Title.

PS8563 E6257 G66 2018   jC813'.6   C2017-902914-2
                                                 C2017-902915-0

Published simultaneously in the United States of America by Tundra Books of Northern New York, an imprint of Penguin Random House Canada Young Readers, a Penguin Random House Company

Library of Congress Control Number: 2017940269

Edited by Tara Walker
Designed by Jennifer Griffiths
The artwork in this book was rendered in pastels and colored pencils.
The text was handlettered by Geneviève Godbout.

Printed and bound in China

www.penguinrandomhouse.ca

1   2   3   4   5   22   21   20   19   18

Penguin
Random House
TUNDRA BOOKS

Goodnight, Anne

INSPIRED BY ANNE OF GREEN GABLES

Written by KALLIE GEORGE

Illustrated by GENEVIÈVE GODBOUT

tundra

Time for bed, Anne.

Yes, Marilla, but not before I say goodnight.
I always say goodnight to everyone I love.

Goodnight, Matthew, shy and sweet.

Thank you *so* much for the dress with *real* puffed sleeves.

Goodnight, Diana, my bosom friend.

We were kindred spirits
the moment we met.

Goodnight, Gilbert.
Well, really, good riddance.

I will *never* forgive you
for calling me Carrots!

But I forgave Mrs. Rachel Lynde, and she forgave me.

We both speak our minds and should mind what we say.

So goodnight, Mrs. Lynde, dear nosy neighbor.

And goodnight, Miss Stacy,
my splendid teacher.

(When she says my name,
I just *know* she's spelling Anne
with an *e*.)

Goodnight, Bonny, growing on the sill.

Everything deserves its own name.

And Bonny is a much better name
than just geranium, isn't it?

Goodnight, my Snow Queen, all dressed in white.

Listen . . . can you hear her talking in her sleep?
What nice dreams trees must have!

Goodnight, Lake of Shining Waters.

Oh, you always seem to be smiling at me!

Goodnight, sky and bright,
clear stars.

If you could live on a star,
which one would you choose?

Or would you rather live in a tree?
I do *love* trees.

A wild cherry would make
a wonderful bed.

Anne Shirley, time for *your* bed.

Yes, Marilla, sensible and strict.

Sometimes, oh, how much you miss!

But goodnight, Marilla.

I love you so.

Goodnight to *all* of my kindred spirits.

And goodnight, Green Gables.

You really are the dearest, loveliest spot in the world.
As soon as I saw you, I *knew* I was home.

Goodnight, Avonlea.

Goodnight, Island.

Goodnight to this whole dear old world.

Time to sleep.

Time to dream . . .

Goodnight, Anne.

Anne with an e.